Billie B. Brown

www.BillieBBrownBooks.com

Billie B. Brown Books

The Bad Butterfly
The Soccer Star
The Midnight Feast
The Second-best Friend
The Extra-special Helper
The Beautiful Haircut
The Big Sister
The Spotty Vacation
The Birthday Mix-up
The Secret Message
The Little Lie
The Best Project
The Deep End
The Copycat Kid
The Night Fright
The Bully Buster
The Missing Tooth
The Book Buddies

First American Edition 2013
Kane Miller, A Division of EDC Publishing

Text copyright © 2010 Sally Rippin
Illustrations copyright © 2010 Aki Fukuoka
Logo and design copyright © 2010 Hardie Grant Egmont

First published in Australia in 2010 by Hardie Grant Egmont

For information contact:
Kane Miller, A Division of EDC Publishing
P.O. Box 470663
Tulsa, OK 74147-0663
www.kanemiller.com
www.edcpub.com
www.usbornebooksandmore.com

Library of Congress Control Number: 2011935698

Printed and bound in the United States of America
14 15 16 17 18 19 20
ISBN: 978-1-61067-100-2

Billie B. Brown

The Beautiful Haircut

By Sally Rippin

Illustrated by Aki Fukuoka

Kane Miller
A DIVISION OF EDC PUBLISHING

Chapter One

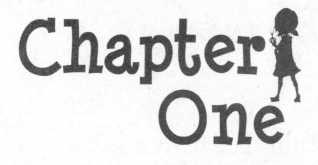

Billie B. Brown has three long-haired dolls, twelve sparkly hair clips and one pink comb. Do you know what the "B" in Billie B. Brown stands for?

Beautiful.

Billie B. Brown is
playing hairdressers today.
Hairdressers make people
look beautiful.

Jack is Billie's best friend.
He lives next door.
Billie and Jack play
together every day.

ox of sparkly
air clips

Three long-haired
dolls

Pink comb

3

If Jack wants to build a fort, Billie helps him. If Billie wants to play soccer, Jack plays too.

But Jack doesn't want to play with Billie today.

"Why don't you want me to do your hair?" Billie asks. "I can make you look beautiful."

"No, thanks," Jack frowns.

"Why not?" asks Billie.

"I am a great hairdresser.
I can make anyone look
beautiful. Long hair,
short hair, boy, girl."

Jack scrunches up his face. "I don't want to look beautiful, Billie. I want to look cool. Can't we play something else?"

"No, I want to play hairdressers," Billie says **crossly**. "If you don't want to play with me you can go home."

Jack stares at Billie.

Billie stares at Jack. Then

Jack stands up and walks

out of Billie's bedroom.

Billie looks out her
bedroom window.
She sees Jack walk outside
into the backyard.

There is a hole in the
fence between Jack's
house and Billie's house.
Jack squeezes through
the hole and runs home.

Billie feels very **annoyed**.

She and Jack always play together! It was Billie's turn to choose the game so she chose hairdressers. Jack didn't even try to let Billie do his hair!

Billie knows Jack will be back soon. They never stay **mad** at each other for long.

Anyway, Billie doesn't have time to **worry** about Jack now. She is a hairdresser, and she has lots of customers!

Chapter Two

Billie looks at her dolls.
They all have long hair.

"I don't need Jack to play
hairdressers," she says
to them. "I have you.
OK, who is next?"

Billie picks up a doll. "Claudia! Look at your hair. It's such a mess! I will fix it for you."

When Billie's doll Claudia was new, she had lovely long hair. Now it is like a yellow bush. Long hair is very difficult to take care of.

You have to brush it
a lot. This can be a little
bit boring.

Billie puts some clips in Claudia's hair. "Mmm, that's better," Billie says. Claudia looks beautiful.

Next it is Tomoko's turn. Tomoko has dark hair just like Billie's. Tomoko's hair used to be shiny and smooth, but one day Billie accidentally dropped some glue in it.

Now one side is smooth,
and one side is knotted.

Not to worry. Billie is
such a good hairdresser
that she can make any
hair look great. She puts
a sparkly clip in
Tomoko's hair.
Yes, that's
much better!

Billie's last doll used to be called Barbara, but now everyone calls her Stinky. Stinky used to have long red curls, but now they are just a teensy bit green.

Billie left Stinky out in the backyard for three whole weeks.

Stinky is still beautiful, but now she is a little bit moldy and, well, a little bit **stinky**.

Stinky looks very pretty with sparkly hair clips in her hair, doesn't she?

The dolls are very good customers. They sit very still, and they don't talk.

Much better than Jack, Billie thinks.

But soon Billie starts to get bored. Billie is a very good hairdresser, but real hairdressers don't just put clips in hair.

They don't just brush and comb and smooth.

Real hairdressers **cut**.

Billie looks for her purple plastic scissors in her pencil case. Billie's scissors are very good at cutting paper. She hopes they will be good at cutting hair too.

Billie puts Claudia on
her special hairdressing
seat. She tries to cut
a little bit off the bottom
of Claudia's hair.
But nothing happens.

She tries Tomoko next, and then Stinky. But it's no good.

Billie's plastic scissors are good for cutting paper, but terrible for cutting hair.

Billie frowns. How can she be a hairdresser if she can't even cut hair?

Then, Billie has an idea.

Chapter Three

Billie goes into the
bathroom. She opens
up the drawer and sees a
shiny pair of scissors.

Billie is not allowed to
touch the kitchen scissors.

But these scissors are different, Billie decides. They are only little scissors. Perfect for giving little haircuts.

Billie thinks she is probably allowed to use these.

Billie picks up the little scissors.

She hopes they will be better than her purple plastic ones. They look very sharp. She decides to test them out.

Billie holds up one of her pigtails and gives a little snip.

Oh yes, they are very sharp. Billie's pigtail falls into the sink! It lies there looking like a little furry mouse.

Oh dear. Billie looks in the mirror. Now she only has one pigtail.

Billie doesn't look beautiful at all. In fact, she looks silly! She can't walk around with just one pigtail. Everyone will laugh at her!

So Billie snips off the other pigtail. Now both sides look the same.

Two little pigtails lie in the sink.

Billie is amazed at how easily they came off. She wishes she could stick them back on again. Billie liked her two pigtails. Now she has none!

Billie looks in the mirror. Tears roll down her cheeks. She wishes she had never found those horrible sharp scissors!

She wishes she had her two little pigtails back! She stares at her funny haircut and tries to stop crying.

Just then, Billie sees someone else in the mirror. It's Jack!

"Billie! What have you done?" says Jack.

His eyes are as big as tennis balls. "You cut off your pigtails!"

Billie covers her hair with her hands. "Don't tell Mom!" she pleads. "I'm going to be in so much trouble!"

"But what are you going to do?" asks Jack. "You can't hide your hair forever!"

"I'll wear a hat!" says Billie.

"Until it grows back."

"Don't be silly," Jack says.
"You have to tell your
mom. She'll know what
to do."

Billie hangs her head.
She knows that Jack
is right. She feels very
nervous. But with Jack
beside her, it's not so bad.

They walk into the
kitchen to find Billie's
mom.

Chapter Four

Billie's mom is sitting at the table reading the paper. She looks up as Billie and Jack come into the room. "Oh, Billie!" she gasps. "What have you done?"

Billie scrunches up
her face. She covers her
eyes with her hands.
Then she starts to cry.

"I was playing hairdressers," she sobs.

Billie's mom stands up and pulls Billie into a hug. "My silly Billie," she sighs. She ruffles Billie's funny hair.

"You're not cross?" Billie asks. She looks up at her mom with wet eyes.

"Well, yes, a little bit," Billie's mom frowns. "You know you're not allowed to play with scissors!"

"I know," says Billie glumly. "I'm sorry."

But then Billie's mom gives a small smile. "Do you know what?" she says.

"When I was a little girl I did exactly the same thing." She gives Billie a squeeze.

"Really?" Billie asks, amazed. "You cut off your pigtails?"

"Yep. Except I looked much worse than you," Billie's mom laughs.

"My hair was sticking up everywhere! You've still got plenty of hair left. But it looks like we'll have to take you to a real hairdresser."

"I miss my pigtails," Billie sighs.

"Don't worry," Billie's mom says.

"Glenda will give you a great haircut. She can make anyone look beautiful!"

"Can she do cool haircuts too?" Jack asks.

"You bet," says Billie's mom.

"Great!" says Jack. "Then I'll ask my mom if I can get one too."

"Let's go, then," says
Billie's mom.

Billie hugs her mom.
Jack was right, she thinks.
Mom did know what to do.